Disney
Tangled
The Series

TALES OF RAPUNZEL 3

Friends and Enemies

For Paula and Stan
—K.M.

randomhousekids.com

ISBN 978-0-7364-3830-8 (trade)—
ISBN 978-0-7364-3831-5 (lib. bdg.)

Printed in the United States of America

10 9 8 7 6 5 4 3 2 1

DISNEY
Tangled
The Series

TALES OF RAPUNZEL 3

Friends
and
Enemies

Adapted by
Kathy McCullough

Illustrated by
the Disney Storybook Art Team

 Random House New York

Tale One
Max's Enemy

Maximus paraded through the Corona marketplace, his head held high. Life was good, he thought. He was the top horse in the Corona royal guard and was known throughout the kingdom for his role in helping to rescue Princess Rapunzel from the tower. She had been held prisoner there for almost eighteen years.

Max nodded to the Corona citizens as they greeted him with cheers of admiration. Yes, life was good. The only thing that could make it better was if Max had another horse to pal around with.

Max passed Princess Rapunzel. She was visiting the market with her boyfriend, Eugene, and Eugene's friend Lance, who had recently moved to Corona. "Max, if this were a popularity contest, you'd come in first place," said Rapunzel.

Eugene nodded in agreement. "And your mane looks great," he told Max. "That's coming from someone who knows good hair." Eugene waved to Rapunzel's blond hair, which hung down her back in a long, twisty braid.

Max's mane was braided as well, in a special knotted design.

"Max has to look his best," Rapunzel explained. "He has an important assignment coming up. He'll be pulling the cart full of gold coins to the kingdom's depository." The depository was a secret bank vault that lay

outside the castle walls. It was heavily guarded, but thieves sometimes tried to steal the gold while it was being transported.

Luckily, the cart carrying the gold coins was protected by bars and locks. And ever since Max had taken over the job of pulling the cart, no thief had succeeded in robbing it. Max could outrun any crook and was strong enough to fight the bad guys off with a single kick.

Suddenly, a voice rang out. "Stop! Thief!"

Max glanced around, startled. Where had the cry come from?

"There he is!" cried Rapunzel, pointing toward a man dashing through the crowded marketplace with a purse clutched under his arm. At the edge of the square, the owner of the purse waved her arms in distress.

Max snorted. No thief would get away on

his watch! As he reared up on his hind legs, he heard Rapunzel shout, "Go get him, Max!" Max galloped across the market square. Within seconds, he had closed in on the thief.

Just as Max was about to grab the thief, a flash of black charged in front of him. It was another horse! The horse barreled into the thief, knocking him to the ground. Max leaned on his heels and screeched to a stop. The villagers burst into applause. The captain of the royal guard rushed to the horse, who now had the thief dangling from his jaws. "Brilliantly done!" the captain told the mysterious hero. Max neighed in agreement.

Eugene and Lance hurried over to help. When they grabbed hold of the man, they immediately recognized him: it was Dwayne, a bandit they'd known when they'd been thieves themselves. Eugene had given up his life of crime for Rapunzel. Lance, who had spent several years in prison, was also doing his best to become a law-abiding citizen.

"I've never seen such an impressive horse," the captain said.

The horse was indeed handsome, with a sleek, dark coat and a stylish, spiky mane. His eyes were like black opals and had a silvery shimmer.

Rapunzel noticed a nameplate around the horse's neck. It read "Axel."

"Where's your owner, Axel?" Rapunzel asked the horse.

Axel whinnied and shook his head, making it clear he was all alone in the world.

Rapunzel patted his shoulder. "You can stay at the castle tonight," she told him. Max nodded. It was the least they could do for an orphaned horse who had shown such courage.

"Tomorrow we'll find you a good home," the captain promised Axel. "In the meantime, Max, why don't you show your new pal around?"

Max let out a friendly neigh and nodded for Axel to follow him back to the castle.

* * *

Max thought Axel might be hungry, so he led him to a trough near the stables. In the trough were two stacks of hay. Max nodded to one, offering it to Axel. Axel instantly gobbled down the hay—then devoured Max's as well.

Max tried not to get angry. He reminded himself that Axel had probably been wandering for days before he arrived in Corona. Who knew when the poor horse had last eaten?

After lunch, Max led Axel out to the pretty Corona countryside beyond the village. In a small field, a horse named Fidella grazed beneath a tree.

Max blushed. He had a crush on Fidella, who was also a member of the royal guard. He always felt shy around her, but today he had the urge to show off in front of Axel.

Max plucked a pretty purple flower from a nearby bush and trotted toward Fidella. But before he'd gotten halfway there, Axel walked past him with two flowers in his teeth.

Max raced back to the bush and plucked *three* flowers. Suddenly, Axel appeared next to him and yanked the entire bush out of the ground. Axel galloped to Fidella and dropped the bush at her feet.

Max spit out his flowers. He had a feeling Axel wasn't the kind of "pal" he'd been hoping for.

Max was relieved when night finally came. The next morning, Axel would be taken to a new home, and Max would never have to see him again.

They still had to share a stall for the night, though.

Axel plopped down in the middle of the stall, hogging all the soft straw. He was soon fast asleep, his legs flung in every direction.

Max sighed and stepped into the remaining narrow space. He leaned against the wall and slept standing up.

The next morning, Max stumbled out of the stables, tired and stiff. His head drooped, his eyes were bloodshot, and his mane was a tangled mess. He barely blinked when he saw Axel once again gobbling down all the breakfast hay in the trough.

"There you are, Max!" the captain of the guard called out. "I've been looking for you!"

Max shook off his weariness and stood at attention. No matter how tired or hungry he was, he was still the chief horse of the royal guard. Whatever important duty the captain had for him, Max was ready.

"As you know, Max, we were going to find Axel a home today," said the captain. Max nodded. "But considering his hard work in capturing the thief yesterday, and seeing how inseparable you two have already become, I've decided he should stay." The captain patted Axel's shoulder. "Welcome the newest horse on the royal guard!"

Max gaped in shock. Axel smirked at him— then winked.

CHAPTER 2

Later that morning, while the captain was outside, Max snuck into his office. Pascal, Rapunzel's pet chameleon, sat on Max's back.

When Max was a young colt, he'd dreamed of becoming a member of the royal guard. But wanting it wasn't enough. Before he'd been able to join, he'd had to pass a series of tests.

Max was sure the rules for joining the royal guard were written down somewhere. He needed a bit of help to find them, though, and Pascal was the perfect helper.

Max trotted over to a set of bookshelves, and Pascal leaped onto the top shelf. There the chameleon found the rulebook, and pushed it to a table. Pascal hopped down and flipped through the book. Max neighed when Pascal reached the right page.

Rapunzel passed by the office door and peered in. "There you guys are." She stepped inside. "So, Max. Are you excited Axel is joining the force?"

Max slapped his hoof on the book in response.

Rapunzel picked up the book. "Hmm," she said. She thought Max wanted his new friend to join him on the guard—but he wanted to

make sure it was done "by the book" so nobody could ever say Axel wasn't a *true* guard horse.

Rapunzel brought the book out to the captain in the stables. Max and Pascal followed. The captain took the book and nodded. "Max is right," he said, turning to Axel. "You'll have to pass several tests showing your strength and skill before you can join the guard."

Max gave Axel a triumphant look. Axel wasn't a trained horse—he was sure to fail. Then Max would *finally* be rid of him.

But Axel didn't seem worried. . . .

Rapunzel, Eugene, Lance, and several others gathered in a field behind the stables to watch Axel try out for the guard.

Pete and Stan, two of the royal guards, stood next to Max.

"That Axel's some horse, huh?" Stan said to Max.

"He's a lot like you, Max," said Pete. "But younger."

"And bigger," Stan added. "And tough-looking—which probably means he's stronger, too."

Max glared at both guards, but their eyes were on Axel.

The first test measured how high a horse could reach. Reaching high was helpful for leaping over steep walls during chases and rescues.

The captain stood on a ladder on one side of a twenty-foot wall. Axel waited on the ground on the other side. Max had set a new record when he'd first taken this test. There was a mark on the wall showing how high he had reached.

"Okay, Axel," the captain called down. Axel

reared up on his hind legs and pointed his forelegs skyward. His hooves landed just below Max's mark. Max smiled. But Axel stretched higher and reached his nose past the line, beating Max's record.

The crowd let out gasps of amazement.

"Did he just break Max's record?" Pete asked Stan.

"I can't believe it!" exclaimed Stan. "I didn't think *anyone* would ever break his record!"

As far as Max was concerned, no one would. He galloped over to the wall and leaped onto his hind legs. He stretched his forelegs up, up, up, reaching his nose to the line the captain had drawn for Axel.

Suddenly, Max felt himself tipping backward. He lost his balance and fell, landing—*THUD*—right on his behind.

As he scrambled up from the ground, Max heard snickering from the crowd—and from Axel.

Rapunzel rushed over to him. "What are you doing, Max?" she asked. "You're already on the guard!"

Max knew this, but he couldn't help himself. He hated being outdone.

The next test was about strength.

Axel once again broke Max's record by lifting a two-hundred-pound weight in his teeth. Furious, Max snatched up the weight, spun around, and let the weight go. It flew through the air and crashed into a row of bushes.

The rest of the afternoon, after every test Axel passed, Max tried to prove he was still the strongest, smartest, most skillful horse in the kingdom.

Finally, they reached the last test: aim. Axel had to kick a target hanging from the top of a pole. He jumped into the air, performed a backflip, and easily kicked the target with his rear hooves, hitting the bull's-eye.

While the crowd was applauding Axel, Max ran up and did a flip. He kicked at the target—but hit the pole instead, snapping it in two.

The crowd gasped.

The captain of the guard frowned at him. "At least *Axel* made a good showing today," he said. Max hung his head in embarrassment.

Rapunzel brushed bits of broken pole off Max's back. "You don't have to be the best at *everything*," she told him.

That didn't make Max feel better.

"Yeah, you don't have to be the best," echoed Pete. "Because Axel is."

This made Max feel worse.

The captain patted Axel's neck. "Congratulations, Axel. You're now a member of the royal guard!"

Axel winked at Max.

20

But Max wasn't ready to give up. He dragged a hoof through the dirt, making a bold straight line.

"Well, well, well!" declared the captain when he saw it. "Looks like we have an old-fashioned challenge here!"

Max snorted at Axel.

Once again, Axel didn't seem worried.

The two horses lined up at one side of the field. The captain pointed into the distance. "First to that tree on the other side of the ravine wins," he told them.

The captain blew his whistle and the horses took off. Axel dashed ahead to take the lead, but Max caught up to him as they approached the narrow rope bridge that hung across the ravine.

Moments before they reached the bridge,

21

Axel rammed into Max, shouldering him aside. Max lost his footing and slid over the edge of the ravine, plunging into the muddy ditch below.

On the opposite side of the bridge, Axel cantered and high-stepped, showing off as he reached the tree. Axel caught Max's eye and winked as he tapped his hoof against the tree trunk. He was the winner! The crowd cheered.

Max pushed himself up from the mud and scowled.

Filthy and forlorn, Max trudged back to the castle. There was no way this day could get any worse.

"Max!" the captain of the guard called. "Just the horse I wanted to see!"

Max perked up. At least he was still number one in the captain's eyes.

"I'm worried about you, buddy," the captain told him. "I think you need a rest—which is why I'm having Axel make the trip to the depository tomorrow."

Max was stunned. He wasn't number one anymore!

He'd been replaced.

CHAPTER 3

That night, Max once again slept standing up while Axel hogged the floor.

Max fidgeted, restless. The race with Axel crept into his dreams. . . .

Max tried to charge ahead, but his hooves became stuck, as if the ground had turned to glue. When Axel raced ahead, Fidella appeared, with a white veil over her mane. Axel reached her and a minister stepped forward. He recited wedding vows for the two horses.

Max, horrified, struggled in the gluey dirt.

He finally burst free, sending his body high into the air. . . .

Max tumbled through space, landing in the middle of the Corona marketplace. Axel appeared, pulling a cart piled high with captured thieves. Axel delivered the cart to the captain of the guard as the crowd cheered.

"With the arrest of these bad guys, you've proven yourself the most valuable horse in Corona!" the captain told Axel. "You can have Max's job—and his stall. In fact, you can even have Maximus's name!" The captain hung a shiny new gold nameplate around Axel's neck.

No one noticed Max. He felt a tug—there were now reins around his neck. He was wearing a party hat and pulling a baby in a wagon.

Not only had Max been replaced by Axel, he wasn't even a member of the royal guard anymore!

Max couldn't let that happen. He yanked free of his reins and raced back to the castle.

Just as Max arrived at the castle gates, they slammed shut in his face. Rapunzel leaned over the top of the castle wall and pointed down at him. "Worst. Horse. Ever!" she shouted.

Rapunzel's words echoed over and over in Max's ears. They blended with the strange sound of hooves digging in the dirt. . . .

Max opened his eyes. He was back in his stall. It was only a dream. He still heard the sound of digging, however. He glanced around, but there was no one else there. Axel was gone.

Max peered out from his stall. A moment later, Axel emerged from a nearby stall and slipped into the night. Max quietly followed.

It was too dark outside to see where Axel had gone, but Max put his nose to the ground and sniffed. He followed the scent of Axel's hoof prints to the castle.

Inside the castle, Max heard a light *clip-clop* coming from a nearby hallway. He peeked around the corner and spotted Axel carrying a

large canvas sack in his teeth. A gold coin fell from the sack, landing on the stone floor with a faint *clink*.

Aha! Proof at last that Axel was up to no good!

A few minutes later, Max led Rapunzel and the captain of the guard down the hallway to the fallen coin. Pascal sat on Rapunzel's shoulder, still half asleep.

Max pointed to the coin with his hoof.

"*This* is why you woke me up, Maximus?" demanded the captain.

Axel appeared at the opposite end of the hall, carrying another sack of coins. Max charged over to him and grabbed the bag in his teeth. Axel refused to let go, and the two horses yanked on the bag in a fierce tug-of-war. The

bag ripped open and gold coins poured out, scattering across the stone floor.

Max turned to the captain and Rapunzel, waiting for congratulations on catching the thief.

"You think Axel is stealing money?" the captain asked. Max nodded. The captain shook his head. "Max, he's loading the cart for the trip to the depository—and now he's got to pick up all these coins, thanks to you."

Rapunzel gave Axel a hug. "Sorry about this, Axel," she said. Axel glanced at Max over Rapunzel's shoulder and winked.

Furious, Max rose on his hind legs and neighed loudly. He charged toward Axel, but

Rapunzel threw out her arms, halting him in his tracks. "Stop!" she shouted. "Leave poor Axel alone!"

Rapunzel marched up to Max and folded her arms. "I'm going back to bed, Max, and you need to do the same." She pointed toward the door. *"Now."*

Max trudged off to the stables, defeated.

The next morning, Max snuck out early. He couldn't bear to watch Axel take his place as the official transporter of the gold-filled armored cart.

Max entered the Corona marketplace, but no one noticed him. It felt like his nightmare come to life. Then, to make things worse, it began to rain.

Max ducked under a nearby awning. He

could fit only his head under it, so the rain battered the rest of his body.

Below the awning was the village bulletin board, covered in posters. One was an ad seeking a horse to pull hayride carts for kids.

This was *definitely* Max's nightmare come to life.

Max sighed. He might as well apply for the job. Axel was clearly the top horse now. There was no longer a place for Max in the royal guard.

Max ripped a tag off the bottom of the ad with his teeth. An eye peered out at him from underneath the gap.

Max was startled for a moment, but then he realized it wasn't a real eye. It was a drawing.

Max looked closer. There was something very familiar about that eye. . . .

Max yanked down the hayride ad, revealing a Wanted poster of a masked man riding a masked horse. Despite the masks, Max instantly recognized the man as Dwayne, the thief Axel had nabbed in the marketplace—and the masked horse was none other than Axel!

WANTED

THEFT
CIVIL UNREST
HARASSMENT

Max snatched the poster from the bulletin board and galloped back to the castle, his hooves splashing through the puddles. Max hadn't left the royal guard yet! And he still had a job to do: stop Axel from taking off with the kingdom's money.

Max reached the stables, but there was no sign of Axel anywhere. He remembered hearing Axel digging in one of the stalls. He hurried to the stall and scraped away the hay, looking for Axel's hiding place.

Suddenly, the ground dropped open and Max fell—he'd stepped into a trap!

He heard a snicker coming from above and looked up to see Axel lean over the edge of the trap and wink. Max neighed angrily, but there was nothing he could do. He was imprisoned by high walls on all sides.

Max listened to Axel's hooves fading away and pawed at the dirt. He'd failed again. Now there was no doubt about it: Max didn't deserve to be on the royal guard.

Eugene and Lance watched as Rapunzel paced back and forth in Eugene's room. She was thinking about Max and how oddly he'd been behaving since Axel had arrived. Pascal paced alongside her on the floor.

"I don't get it," Rapunzel said. "Max has no reason not to like Axel."

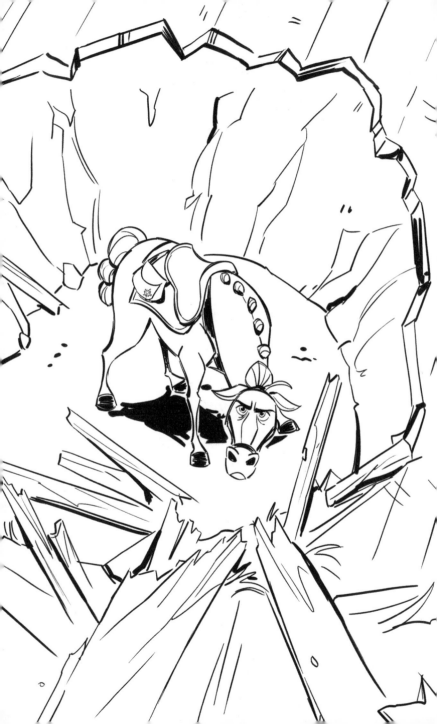

"Or does he?" asked Lance.

Rapunzel looked at Lance, confused.

"Back in the orphanage, we had a hopscotch court," Lance told her. "I was the best. I could hop, skip, and jump. *No one* could out-scotch me. They called me the Sweet Feet Champ. You remember that, Eugene?"

Eugene and Lance had grown up together in the same orphanage. "I remember you called *yourself* that," Eugene said.

Lance frowned at Eugene. "The *important* thing is, the other kids loved me . . . until *she* showed up." A dark look came over Lance's face. "We just knew her as Big Hops. She could hop from one to ten in a single bound. I grew to dislike her because once Big Hops hit the scene, it was like Sweet Feet never existed."

"Just because a new horse came to town

doesn't make Max any less special," Rapunzel said.

Pascal gave her a knowing look—and suddenly Rapunzel understood. It didn't matter what *she* thought. It was what *Max* thought that counted.

And like Lance, Max thought he'd been replaced.

Rapunzel felt awful for scolding Max the night before. "I have to go apologize," she told Eugene and Lance.

Rapunzel entered the stables with Pascal on her shoulder. "Max?" she called. There was no answer.

Pascal spotted a crumpled piece of paper in a corner of the stable. As Rapunzel continued to search for Max, Pascal leaped off her shoulder and ran to the paper. He flattened it out and his eyes went wide. It was the Wanted poster Max had found.

Pascal carried the poster to Rapunzel and pointed to the drawing of the horse. "Is that Axel?" she asked. Pascal nodded.

Suddenly, everything that had happened the last couple of days made sense. "Axel and Dwayne are partners!" exclaimed Rapunzel. "The whole arrest was a set-up!"

A loud neigh sounded from one of the nearby stalls. Rapunzel and Pascal rushed over, pausing at the edge of the stall. Max gazed up at them from inside the trap.

"Don't worry," Rapunzel told him. "We'll get you out of there." There wasn't time to go for help, however. Rapunzel needed to get Max

40

out of the trap, fast. She used her long hair to form a lasso around his stomach, but he was too heavy to lift.

Pascal pointed to a nearby basket brimming with apples. Rapunzel knew how much Max loved apples. She snatched one up and held it out. "Hey, Max! I got your favorite! Come and get it!"

Max sat slumped and silent. Even though he'd barely eaten in two days, he'd lost his appetite.

Rapunzel crouched at the edge of the trap. "You know, Max, when Axel showed up, we thought his size, his strength, and his speed made him the perfect horse," she said. "But we forgot the most important thing—his heart." Max glanced up at her. "You would do anything

for Corona—and for the people in it. No other horse has *half* the heart you do."

Max knew Rapunzel never lied. She wasn't saying this just to get him to come out. She really meant it.

"I'm sorry I didn't believe you about Axel," Rapunzel continued. "You were right all along. And we need *you* to stop him." She stood up.

"Now, what do you say we catch ourselves a horse!"

Max neighed. His fighting spirit had returned. He took a mighty leap, clearing the top of the hole and landing next to Rapunzel.

"You did it, Max!" Rapunzel gave him a big hug. "Unfortunately, I don't know where Axel is," she said. She picked up the Wanted poster

and pointed to the drawing of Dwayne. "But I do know where *he* is."

Rapunzel was right. Dwayne was in the dungeon.

But not for long.

After leaving Max in the trap, Axel had snuck down to the dungeon. He lifted the keys to the cells from their hook on the wall, but he didn't go to Dwayne's cell. He went to the one next to it.

"Hello, Axel," said a female voice from behind the bars. A woman with dark hair and sharp, piercing eyes stepped forward and smiled at her rescuer. The woman was Lady Caine.

A few months earlier, Lady Caine, in disguise, had attended Princess Rapunzel's coronation. With a gang of criminals, she had tried to kidnap Rapunzel's parents, King Frederic and

Queen Arianna. Rapunzel had come to the rescue, using her long blond hair as a weapon. With the help of Eugene and Cassandra, her friend and lady-in-waiting, Rapunzel had stopped Lady Caine and saved her parents.

Lady Caine was Axel's true owner. She, Dwayne, and Axel had come up with this scheme to steal the kingdom's gold if their original plot failed.

And so far, everything was going according to plan. . . .

Rapunzel, Max, and Pascal raced to the castle. When they reached the dungeon, they discovered two empty cells. They quickly put the pieces together and realized that Lady Caine, Dwayne, and Axel were working as a team.

Rapunzel ran outside and looked around for the armored cart, but it was gone—along with the three thieves. She and Max exchanged a glance. They both knew there was only one thing to do.

Rapunzel leaped onto Max's back. With Pascal cheering them on, Rapunzel and Max sped off through the castle gates. They galloped into the marketplace and down the village streets.

Finally, they caught sight of Axel and the armored cart on a road outside the village.

"Come on, Max!" Rapunzel yelled. "We've almost got 'em!" Max lowered his head and broke into a gallop. His legs were moving so fast, they were a blur.

Lady Caine peered through the bars at the rear of the cart. She and Dwayne had hidden inside with the bags of gold. She spotted Rapunzel and Max over the top of a hill. "Looks like we've got company!" She pushed open the hatch in the cart, climbed onto the roof, and

raised the sword Axel had stolen for her from one of the guards. "Show them what a *real* horse can do!" she called down to Axel.

Axel charged ahead—but Max put on another burst of speed and pulled up alongside the cart.

Lady Caine swung her sword toward Rapunzel. Max veered away just in time, keeping the princess clear of the blade.

Rapunzel unbraided her hair and whipped it toward Lady Caine, knocking the sword out of her hand.

"Don't worry, Lady Caine," Dwayne shouted from inside the cart. "I'm coming!" He climbed through the hatch to the roof.

"Sorry, Dwayne," Lady Caine said. "Time to lose the deadweight!" Then she callously shoved him off the cart.

Panicked, Dwayne reached out and managed to grab Rapunzel's hair, pulling her off Max. He and Rapunzel crashed into a row of bushes next to the road.

Max slowed, but Rapunzel waved him on. "I'm okay!" she called. "Go get the other two!"

Max raced ahead. Axel saw Max approaching and began to chew through his harness.

"What are you doing?" cried Lady Caine. Axel ignored her. The reins snapped in two and the cart veered off the road. "You traitor!" Lady Caine yelled as Axel disappeared down the path.

Max saw the cart speeding toward a tree. It was moving too quickly for Lady Caine to jump off safely. Max had no choice. He had to save Lady Caine from certain death. He hurried to grab the rear hitch with his teeth, stopping the cart seconds before it smashed into the tree.

Lady Caine stared at Max in amazement. "You saved my life," she said. "You know, if you're looking for a job, I happen to need a new horse."

A rope of long blond hair appeared out of nowhere. It wrapped around Lady Caine, pinning her arms to her sides.

Rapunzel yanked Lady Caine off the cart. Behind Rapunzel, Eugene and Lance appeared. They'd seen her and Max speed away from the

castle and had quickly followed. They hauled Dwayne out of the bushes.

"We've got these two covered," Rapunzel told Max. Max nodded and raced after Axel, who had paused at the top of a hill to catch his breath. "Go get 'im, Max!" he heard Rapunzel call behind him.

Axel saw Max coming and took off down the other side of the hill, toward a ravine. Max caught up as Axel headed for a narrow log connecting the gap. Just as Axel leaned toward Max to shove him, Max leaped into the air and did a backflip, causing Axel to lose his balance.

Max landed at the edge of the ravine—in time to see Axel tumble into the mud below. *SPLAT!*

Max peered down at Axel. When Axel scowled

up at him, Max snickered—and winked.

By this time, the royal guards had discovered the criminals' escape and had arrived on the scene. They'd already arrested Dwayne and Lady Caine, and now they climbed down into the ravine to arrest Axel.

Rapunzel hurried to Max and hugged him. The captain of the guard joined them and patted Max's back. "Brilliantly done, Maximus!" the captain said. "You're one of a kind!"

Rapunzel hugged Max again. "You really are the best horse in the kingdom," she said.

Max neighed in reply. He felt good about stopping Axel. But the true triumph of the day was realizing how many genuine friends he had in Corona—from the smallest chameleon to the princess of the whole kingdom. The royal

guard wasn't just his job—it was his home, and the people in the castle were his family.

Rapunzel climbed onto Max's back and whispered in his ear. "I think there's an apple cart back at the castle with your name on it."

Apples! Max's eyes went wide. He'd worked up quite an appetite chasing Axel, and he was starving! He took off like a shot, with Rapunzel clinging to his back, leaving the others in the dust.

The captain watched Max and Rapunzel vanish down the road. He shook his head in admiration. "Now *that's* how you do it!" he exclaimed. Eugene and Lance nodded in agreement. If this had been a race, it seemed certain Max would have set another record.

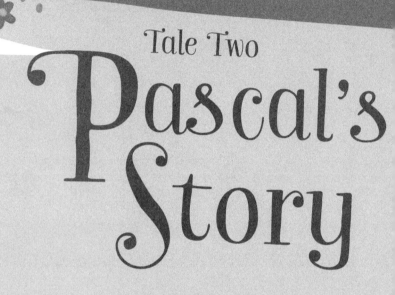

Tale Two

Pascal's Story

Pascal was fast asleep on his little branch suspended over Rapunzel's bed in the castle. Usually his dreams were happy ones, about whatever he and Rapunzel had done together that day. Things like chasing each other through the castle hallways, playing hide-and-seek, or doing a jigsaw puzzle.

But tonight his dreams took him back in time, to long before he lived in the castle. Before he even knew Rapunzel . . .

Baby Pascal clung to his mother's tail as she

61

raced through a field. There was a rustle in the grass behind them. Pascal glanced back and saw flashes of red and black stripes moving along the ground.

A head rose from the grass—it was a snake! It flicked its tongue at Pascal as it slithered closer.

Pascal's mother hurried on, until she reached a riverbank. She gently placed Pascal on a large leaf, kissed his tiny head, and pushed the leaf out onto the river.

Pascal floated away from shore. His mother turned back to fight the snake, but he lost sight of her as the river carried the leaf forward. A few moments later, the leaf tumbled over a waterfall and splashed into a pond.

The leaf drifted to shore and Pascal hopped off. He climbed up the rocky bank to a

forest and wandered among the tall
trees until he came to a small
cave. He ducked inside—and
discovered it was actually a
tunnel. As he emerged into a
clearing, he heard singing. It
was the voice of a young girl.
The sound was coming from a
tall tower in the distance.
The song she sang
was so pretty

and her voice was so sweet, Pascal was sure she would help him. He hurried to the tower and climbed up the stones to the single window at the top.

But Pascal had been followed! Just as Pascal hopped through the windowsill, the snake rose behind him and clamped its fangs into Pascal's shoulder. The sting from the bite spread and he grew dizzy.

The last thing Pascal saw before everything went black was a giant frying pan whisking over his head and smashing into the snake, breaking off one of its fangs.

The snake flew out the window as Pascal collapsed.

When Pascal woke up, he once again heard singing. It was the same song he'd heard in the forest: "Flower, gleam and glow. Let your power shine. . . ."

Pascal was wrapped in a lock of the girl's blond hair. The hair gave off a warm glow, and Pascal's shoulder tingled where the snake had bitten him.

The girl finished the song and unwrapped her hair. Pascal glanced at his shoulder—his wound had completely healed!

"You're safe now," the little girl whispered. "I guess you're all alone, huh?" Pascal nodded. "So am I," she said. "Most of the time." She smiled. "I know! You can stay with me! Then neither of us will be alone!" She plucked a pink button off her dress and set it on Pascal's head. "It's a gift! From me to you."

Pascal hugged the button under one arm and climbed up to the girl's shoulder.

The chameleon's happy dream continued. He remembered how he and his new friend Rapunzel had grown up together. They played games,

danced, and cooked. Most of all, they had fun.

Every year on Rapunzel's birthday, she and Pascal would sit in the window of the tower and watch the floating lanterns in the sky in the distance. They didn't know then that the lanterns

were launched by the people of Corona. King Frederic and Queen Arianna had started the tradition after Rapunzel had been kidnapped by evil Mother Gothel. The king and queen hoped the lanterns would lead Rapunzel home . . . and eventually, they did.

But even before that happened, Rapunzel and Pascal were happy because they had each other. Every night before they went to sleep, Rapunzel would tell Pascal, "You'll always be my best friend."

Back in the castle, Pascal woke up with a smile on his face. He glanced down from his branch, hoping to share his dream with Rapunzel—but her bed was empty.

Pascal's smile faded. Since they'd moved to the castle, Rapunzel still told Pascal every night that he was her best friend.

But he was no longer her *only* friend.

Pascal found Rapunzel in the kitchen, making soup. She liked to make soup early in the day so the flavors had time to blend by dinner. They'd learned this in the tower, where they'd gotten very good at making delicious soups with whatever ingredients Mother Gothel brought them.

Pascal was Rapunzel's official taste-tester. She counted on him to tell her when a soup needed more of something or was perfect as it was.

"Pascal!" Rapunzel said when she saw him. "Thank goodness you're here!" She lifted him

onto her shoulder and offered him a spoonful of soup. Pascal slurped it—delicious! He gave her a thumbs-up.

Eugene appeared over Rapunzel's other shoulder and grabbed the spoon, taking a taste. "Could use a touch more balsamic vinegar," he said. He added a couple of drops to the pot, stirred the soup, and tasted it again. "Mmm! Now, *that's* perfect!"

Eugene forced Pascal to take a sip. Pascal spit it out and scowled. Maybe it *did* taste a *little* better—but Pascal was Rapunzel's official taste-tester! *Not* Eugene.

Luckily, only *two* could play chess. So later, it was just Pascal and Rapunzel in the courtyard, where Rapunzel had set up a game.

Rapunzel moved one of her pawns. Pascal

studied the board a moment, then pushed his castle-shaped rook forward two spaces.

"Nice move, Pascal!" Rapunzel said.

"What?! Congratulating your opponent?!" cried Cassandra as she marched into the courtyard. "Chess is *war*, Rapunzel, and your opponent is the *enemy*."

Cassandra, Rapunzel's lady-in-waiting, had been adopted and raised by the captain of the guard. He'd taught her how to fight and defend

herself, and she was determined to teach these skills to Rapunzel.

"I want you to look at this board with only one thought," Cassandra told her. "*No mercy. Now show me that game face!*"

Rapunzel glared across the board at her imaginary opponent. She seemed to have forgotten Pascal was there. He waved, trying to get her attention.

Rapunzel shooed him away. "Not now, Pascal," she said. "I'm no-mercying my enemy." Since Rapunzel would be queen one day, she needed to know how to be fierce on the battlefield—even if the battlefield was only a chessboard.

Pascal frowned. Apparently, it took only *one* person to play chess.

* * *

Rapunzel couldn't swordfight alone, of course. Pascal joined her that afternoon near the stables to practice.

"I know we're better with frying pans," Rapunzel told him as they each held up their sword. "But swords seem to be the weapon of choice outside the tower."

Rapunzel swung her sword and smacked Pascal's out of his hand. It landed point-down in the dirt. A second later, Max raced over and snatched it with his teeth.

"Aha!" said Rapunzel, delighted. "A new and worthy opponent!" She raised her sword. *"En garde!"* She lunged toward Max and the two clashed swords with glee.

Pascal sighed, once again forgotten. It seemed there was *nothing* Rapunzel needed him for anymore.

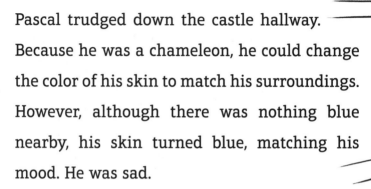

Pascal trudged down the castle hallway. Because he was a chameleon, he could change the color of his skin to match his surroundings. However, although there was nothing blue nearby, his skin turned blue, matching his mood. He was sad.

"All alone again, huh?" Pascal glanced up to see Shorty leaning against the wall. "I know how that goes, believe me," the thug told him.

Shorty was one of the pub thugs, thieves who had helped Eugene rescue Rapunzel from Mother Gothel. They'd given up their criminal ways and were now frequent visitors to the castle.

Shorty was the oldest of the thugs. He could be lazy and forgetful, but he seemed to

understand what Pascal was going through, and Pascal was grateful.

"Sometimes friends can let you down," Shorty continued. Pascal nodded. "But the key to that door is to not let it *keep* you down."

Shorty didn't always make sense, but he did now. He was telling Pascal to not let anything get in the way of his friendship with Rapunzel.

Pascal's skin returned to its natural green. He threw back his tiny shoulders.

"That's what I'm talking about!" Shorty cheered. "Now go out there and do that thing!"

Pascal saluted Shorty and marched off, determined to find *something* he and Rapunzel could do together, just the two of them.

Pascal got up early the next morning and went to work. By the time Rapunzel woke up, her room was filled with supplies for different activities. There were jigsaw puzzles, painting materials, a guitar, and all kinds of flowers to braid in her hair.

Rapunzel gazed around in amazement. "Look at all this!" she exclaimed. "You planned the whole day for us? How fun!"

Pascal beamed. Shorty had been right. Pascal just had to take charge.

A moment later, Cassandra burst into the room and grabbed Rapunzel's arm. "Hurry up and get dressed! You have breakfast with the duke's daughter in five minutes!"

Rapunzel saw Pascal's face fall. "It's just breakfast," she told him. "But after that—"

"After that, you have to teach an art class to the village children," Cassandra said. "Then you have the council meeting, and after that is the music mix-and-mingle with Hook Foot, and then Audience with the Citizens—you're booked solid *all day*."

Pascal slumped, defeated. He felt his skin growing blue again.

"I'm so sorry, Pascal," Rapunzel told him.

"But let's have dinner tonight! Just you and me. Like old times."

Pascal thought it over. He was still upset he wouldn't see Rapunzel all day, but he liked the "just you and me" part. He nodded.

"Six o'clock," Rapunzel told him. "Promise!"

Pascal spent the whole afternoon cooking a very special meal for Rapunzel. There were six courses, with all their favorite foods from their days in the tower, from dandelion salad to forest-berry cake. Pascal had the kitchen staff carry the feast to the royal dining table.

The clock struck six. Pascal gazed at the door, excited.

The door did not open.

In the throne room, Rapunzel heard the first *dong* marking the time. It was six o'clock and

she hadn't finished Audience with the Citizens. This was one of Rapunzel's most important jobs as princess. The people of Corona could visit the castle to ask for help or advice, or to offer their ideas for improving the kingdom.

Luckily, she was on her last citizen, a man who had presented her with a long scroll listing suggestions for the official Corona slogan.

"My favorite is 'Corona: Hit Them Where the Sun *Does* Shine,'" the man told Rapunzel.

"They're *all* very . . . interesting," Rapunzel said.

The man grinned, pleased, and the guards escorted him out.

Rapunzel hopped off her throne. If she rushed, she could get to the dining room before another minute passed.

Just as she reached the door, Shorty burst in, riding a pig. The pig oinked and squealed.

"Your Highness! This pig demands to be heard!" declared Shorty. The pig oinked again. "I will translate for you," Shorty continued, "since I am fluent in pig Latin."

Rapunzel sighed and trudged back to her throne. She glanced at the clock as the pig continued to squeal. She had a feeling this one would take a long time. . . .

Pascal stared at the dining room door and waited. The candlesticks on the table had burned halfway down. When he saw the door handle turn, he perked up. Rapunzel had arrived at last!

But it wasn't Rapunzel who peeked through

the door. It was Lance. He leaned in, taking a big sniff. "I smell stroganoff!" he declared, entering the room. Pascal waved at Lance to leave, but Lance ignored him.

Lance lifted the lids from the different courses, sniffing and smiling. "I'd like to raise a glass to you, Pascal." He picked up a glass. "And lower it." He then flipped the glass upside down on top of Pascal, trapping him. "And say: Reptile, you have *great* taste."

Pascal watched, frustrated, as Lance devoured the meal he'd spent hours cooking. The candlesticks burned down to stubs and the flames went out. When Lance finished the last bite, he laid his head on his arms and went to sleep. His hand knocked into Pascal's glass prison, tipping it over.

The dinner was gone, but Pascal was free. He raced out to the hall to look for Rapunzel. He was sure there was a good reason why she hadn't come. After all, she'd promised, and Rapunzel always kept her promises. He hoped nothing had happened to her.

In another part of the castle, Rapunzel raced down a different hall. She didn't want Pascal's dinner to be ruined.

She passed Eugene, who caught her arm.

"Hey, Blondie!" Eugene said. "What say you and I head over to the canal for a romantic boat ride?"

Rapunzel shook her head. "I'm sorry, Eugene. I promised Pascal I'd have dinner with him—and I'm already late."

Eugene frowned. "Getting ditched for a frog. *Ouch.*"

"Aw . . . are you jealous of Pascal?" Rapunzel pinched Eugene's cheek.

At that moment, Pascal entered the hallway, but neither Rapunzel nor Eugene saw him.

"Don't worry, silly," Rapunzel told Eugene. "You're still my best friend."

Pascal's skin turned gray when he heard this, causing him to blend in with the walls. He slunk away, crushed.

"You're my best friend after *Pascal,* that is," Rapunzel continued.

But Pascal didn't hear *that.* He'd already turned the corner.

Pascal sat on Rapunzel's bed and paged through her journal.

The beginning was filled with pictures of Pascal and Rapunzel in the tower—playing games, making art, gazing out the tower window at the floating lanterns, and being happy together.

But the later pages were different. Pascal was still in a lot of them, but only in the background. There were drawings of Rapunzel with Eugene, with Cassandra, and with the king and queen. Pascal was just a tiny green dot, watching from a distance.

Pascal shoved the journal away, knocking over a jewelry box. The contents spilled to the floor, and among the rings and necklaces, Pascal spotted the pink button Rapunzel had given him the day he arrived at the tower.

Pascal hopped to the floor and picked up the button, hugging it with tears in his eyes.

Rapunzel had promised Pascal he would always be her best friend. He'd thought "always" meant forever, but now he knew that wasn't true.

Rapunzel had many, many friends outside of the tower, and Eugene had become her number one. Pascal was lower on the list. Soon he wouldn't be on the list at all.

Pascal dropped the button to the floor. He crawled up to the windowsill and glanced out at the dark night. There didn't seem to be any reason to stay. No one would miss him. Especially not Rapunzel.

Pascal cast one last look back, then climbed out the window.

CHAPTER 4

"Pascal? Are you in here?"

After finding the dining room empty—except for a snoring Lance—Rapunzel had gone to her bedroom. She'd been sure she'd find Pascal asleep on his branch.

But he wasn't there.

Since then, Rapunzel had been racing up and down the halls, calling for him. Everyone had gone to bed, and her voice echoed off the marble walls. "Pascal!"

No one answered.

Rapunzel rushed into Eugene's room and shook him awake.

"Who? What? Where?" Eugene mumbled. He squinted out from under his sleep mask, confused.

"Pascal's disappeared!" cried Rapunzel.

Eugene pushed the mask to his forehead. "Isn't that his thing?" he asked. "His skin changes color and he blends in, making him disappear. Right?"

"Yes, but—"

"I'm sure he's fine." Eugene pulled his mask down and rolled over.

Rapunzel wasn't sure at all. Yes, Pascal could change his skin color, but he could never hide from *her*. They had spent years playing hide-and-seek in the tower, and she always found him.

Rapunzel yanked the pillow from under Eugene's head. His mask fell off and his eyes snapped open.

"Pascal's never spent the night away from me," Rapunzel told Eugene. She squeezed the pillow, trying not to panic. "What if something's happened to him? What if he's alone and scared and in danger?"

Rapunzel stared down at Eugene, her eyes wide with worry. He was helpless to resist that look. Rapunzel needed him, which meant sleep had to wait.

"I'll get my boots," he said.

Slices of moonlight scattered along the leafy ground as Pascal crept through the dark forest. After leaving the castle, he'd jumped onto a passing hay cart, riding it out of the village

to a country road and jumping off at the edge of the forest. It was a forest he knew, and he hoped he could find the path he'd followed once before. . . .

"Pascal!" Rapunzel called again, as she had been doing for hours. "Where are you? Come out, buddy!" Nearby, Maximus sniffed the castle floors, following Pascal's scent. Max had joined the search and was determined to find his little friend.

When dawn lit up the castle windows, Eugene turned to Rapunzel. "Blondie, are you sure you want to keep—"

Rapunzel whirled around. "Yes! I'm sure I want to keep looking!" Her bloodshot eyes were wild with fear and exhaustion.

"Okay! Okay!" Eugene said quickly. "We'll keep looking!"

Rapunzel followed Max as he sniffed around the plant where Pascal had talked to Shorty the day before.

Eugene noticed Cassandra enter the hallway and hurried over to her. "Are you looking for Rapunzel?" he asked her. "Because I wouldn't. Pascal's disappeared, and we've been searching for him all night. Rapunzel's a little upset, so you might want to—"

Cassandra pushed Eugene aside. "Move it, powder puff," she said.

Eugene shrugged. He'd tried to warn her!

Cassandra tapped Rapunzel's shoulder. "Raps—"

Rapunzel spun around and clutched

Cassandra's arms. "Did somebody find something? Did he turn up? Is he okay?" Her words came out fast, and her fingers squeezed Cassandra's arms so tightly, Cassandra could feel the bruises forming.

"No, I'm sorry," Cassandra said, keeping her voice calm. "I haven't seen Pascal." She peeled Rapunzel's fingers off her arms. "But you have another full day of princess duties ahead, so we need to call off the search."

"What?" cried Rapunzel. "No!"

"Listen, you—"

"*No,*" Rapunzel snapped. "*You* listen. Cancel everything. Lock down the castle. Nothing gets done until we find Pascal. Nothing is more important than that." Rapunzel glanced from Eugene to Cassandra. Her eyes were no longer

wild. They were filled with determination. Her weariness had fled. She was awake and focused. *"Nothing,"* she repeated. "Is that clear?"

Cassandra had never seen Rapunzel more serious—or more frightening. She was truly impressed. "Wow," she said. "Now *that's* a game face."

CHAPTER 5

The sun was high in the sky, and Pascal was hungry and exhausted. He was also lost. He must have gotten turned around in the night and gone in the wrong direction.

He was about to curl up against a rock and close his eyes, when he saw it.

A few feet ahead, between two trees, was the small cave he remembered. Pascal hurried toward it and dashed through, exiting into a clearing. . . .

Ahead of him, rising into the sky, was the tower.

* * *

Rapunzel showed Eugene and Cassandra the Missing poster she'd made. It had a drawing of Pascal and the promise of a trillion gold pieces for his return.

They'd spent all morning and afternoon searching the castle, skipping lunch. The guards had searched the grounds outside, and Max had searched the stables, but Pascal remained missing. Rapunzel knew many Corona citizens had already begun searching the village, but posting the flyer would let *everyone* know.

Eugene studied the flyer. "It's a great drawing of Pascal," he said. "But why did you make him look so terrified?"

"Because he's scared and alone and frightened without me!" Rapunzel answered, clutching the flyer.

When she'd returned to her bedroom to draw the flyer, she'd spotted her journal. It was open to a picture of Rapunzel and Eugene riding Max and playing polo with Cassandra and Fidella. Pascal was just a speck in the background, sitting on a fence and watching the others have fun. Rapunzel was stabbed with guilt, realizing how left out Pascal must have felt.

MISSING!

REWARD
1,000,000,000,000

"He ran away, and it's all my fault," Rapunzel continued. "I've been so busy, I forgot to put our friendship first."

"Don't be so hard on yourself, Blondie," Eugene told her. "He can't have gotten far. He's tiny."

Rapunzel saw Cassandra gathering the fallen jewelry and noticed the pink button. She snatched it up, remembering the day she'd given it to Pascal. It was the day he'd arrived in the tower. The day he'd become her friend—her only friend until they'd moved to the castle . . .

Rapunzel looked up at Eugene and Cassandra. "I know where he is," she told them.

Pascal had climbed to the tower's windowsill, and he now pushed open the shutters. They swung inward with a loud creak. He leaped to

the floor and looked around. It was dark inside, and empty. Yet he felt strangely at home.

He made a fire in the fireplace. The flames cast an orange glow over the objects in the room, bringing back memories of his time there with Rapunzel.

Pascal spotted his old basket bed hanging from a beam, and remembered when Rapunzel had made it for him. He saw pieces of the shattered mirror on the floor, and remembered when they'd stood at that same mirror and made silly faces at each other.

Pascal was so caught up in his memories, he didn't notice a black shadow slip into the room and slither toward him.

Suddenly, there was a loud *HISS!*

Pascal whirled around to find himself face to face with the snake that had attacked him

years before. The snake had followed Pascal to the tower from outside the cave. It had been lurking there all this time, waiting for its chance at revenge.

The snake hissed again and rose to strike. Pascal dashed toward his basket bed, but the snake swatted Pascal with its tail, sending him flying across the room. Pascal smashed into a clay jar, shattering it.

Pascal was stunned for a moment, but he shook it off and raced up the winding staircase

to the room's upper level. He crawled across the banister and jumped to the shelf above the stove.

Pascal ran across the shelf, shoving jars, plates, and pots down at the snake. The snake dodged the falling items as they crashed to the floor.

Pascal spotted a frying pan like the one Rapunzel had used to hit the snake. He struggled to lift it off its hook, but it was too heavy and it slipped through his hands to the floor.

The snake slithered up the stove toward him. The basket bed hung a few feet away, and Pascal jumped, catching the edge.

Below him, the snake snapped its jaws, its single fang inches from Pascal's toes. Pascal clutched the basket and pulled himself up, tumbling into its bed.

The snake bit at the air below him, but Pascal was too high for it to reach. He was safe—but for how long?

Would he be trapped in the basket forever?

CHAPTER 6

Two horses raced through the forest at twilight. The trees around them shimmered in shades of pink and purple.

Rapunzel and Eugene rode Maximus, and Cassandra rode Fidella. The horses galloped as fast as they could, trying to outrun the setting sun. But by the time they made it to the small cave, night had fallen.

They walked through the cave to the clearing, and the sinister shape of the tower rose in the distance. The moonlight shone

behind it, casting a long, thin shadow directly onto Rapunzel.

Rapunzel shivered. This was the first time she'd been back to the tower since she'd escaped. Fear pierced her chest. She felt faint and stumbled backward, but two strong hands caught her and kept her from falling.

The hands belonged to Eugene, and he whispered in her ear. "You don't have to go up there alone, you know."

"Yes, I do." Rapunzel took a deep breath. "I owe it to Pascal."

"If you change your mind . . . Cassandra would be happy to go with you," Eugene said.

Cassandra glared at him, but Rapunzel smiled, grateful to Eugene for lightening the mood. Eugene liked to joke, but Rapunzel could always hear the warmth underneath his words.

She knew he'd stand by her if she needed him.

She stepped forward into the clearing. "Don't be afraid," she told herself. "It's just a tower." Her need to find Pascal and tell him he was still her most important friend pushed her fear to the background.

Rapunzel circled the tower and stepped through the shadows to the entrance to the staircase. When she was growing up in the tower, the entrance had been bricked over. She didn't learn

about it until her last days there. When she'd left with Eugene, she thought she'd never have to see it again. . . .

Inside the tower, Pascal closed his eyes and tried to ignore the sound of the snake below him, hissing and snapping its jaws.

"Pascal?"

Pascal's eyes popped open. It was Rapunzel's voice! Pascal peered over the edge of the basket and saw a faint light coming from the opening in the floor that led to the tower's staircase.

"Pascal? Are you up there?"

The snake had heard the voice, too, and it slithered toward the hole. If Pascal didn't do something quickly, the snake would bite Rapunzel.

Pascal climbed up the basket's rope to the

rafters. He untied the rope and the basket fell to the floor with a thud.

The snake whipped around and slithered to the basket. Pascal changed his skin color to black to blend in with the shadows and silently jumped to the ground. He tiptoed to the snake, grabbed its tail, and hurled it through the air. The snake smashed into a wall and slid to the floor.

"Hello?" Rapunzel's voice was closer now— she was almost to the top of the steps.

Pascal allowed his skin to return to green. The snake spotted him and raced toward him. When it lunged, Pascal changed to black and dashed to the fallen dishes. He flashed from green to black and back to green, luring the snake closer.

The snake rose on its tail and lunged again—

CLANG!

The snake smashed into the frying pan, which Pascal had tipped onto its side. The snake's remaining fang snapped off.

Pascal saw Rapunzel emerge from the staircase and kept the snake focused on him. He snatched the fang and darted to the fireplace. He raised his arms, clutching the fang in his mouth.

With the flames flickering behind him, Pascal looked like a horrible lizard monster. The snake, terrified, backed away.

Suddenly, a large black object swooped toward the snake. It was the frying pan, now held by Rapunzel. She used it to smack the snake, sending it flying out the window—just like she had so many years before.

Pascal collapsed, exhausted. Rapunzel hurried over and scooped him into her hands. She stared at her little pal. He'd risked his life to save hers, even though she'd let him down over the past months. Pascal was a true friend. It broke her heart that he didn't know how important he was to her.

"I know why you came here, Pascal," Rapunzel told him. "Life was so simple when it was just the two of us. But that doesn't mean I don't love you." She lifted him up to her cheek. "*That* will never change."

Rapunzel took the pink button from her pocket and handed it to him. "You will always be my best friend," she promised.

Pascal hugged the button tightly. Tears came to his eyes, but they were tears of happiness.

He was still Rapunzel's best friend—like she was his.

"No one could ever take your place in my heart," said Rapunzel. Pascal nuzzled Rapunzel's cheek, and she smiled. "*Or* on my shoulder."

In Rapunzel's bedroom that night, Pascal watched her add the finishing touches to a new drawing in her journal.

The picture showed Pascal sitting on Rapunzel's shoulder, just as he was now.

Rapunzel closed the journal and placed it on the nightstand. Pascal climbed down her

arm, into his bed on the branch, but Rapunzel quickly plucked him off. "I don't think so!" she said, setting him down on a small pillow next to hers. "Here is better. Right by my side."

Pascal smiled and curled up on the little pillow.

"It wasn't the same without you here," Rapunzel said softly. She kissed Pascal's head. "Good night, Pascal."

Rapunzel pulled up her covers and closed her eyes. Pascal closed his eyes, too. As he drifted off to sleep, next to his best friend, he knew that night's dreams would be happy ones.

Secrets Unlocked

TALES OF RAPUNZEL 1

Opposites Attract

TALES OF RAPUNZEL 2

Friends and Enemies

TALES OF RAPUNZEL 3